Dwight had waited for weeks to go to the baseball game with his Uncle Roy. He loved the Mighty Mustangs.

The night air was cool, and Dwight had his jacket tightly buttoned. "I have my baseball glove," said Dwight, "and my team cap."

2

Dwight and his uncle
found seats near the
outfield. The crowd
started to cheer as
the players took their
places on the field.

The High Flyers were
up first. Their player hit
the ball hard, right into
the glove of the Mustang
first baseman.
"Out!" yelled the umpire.

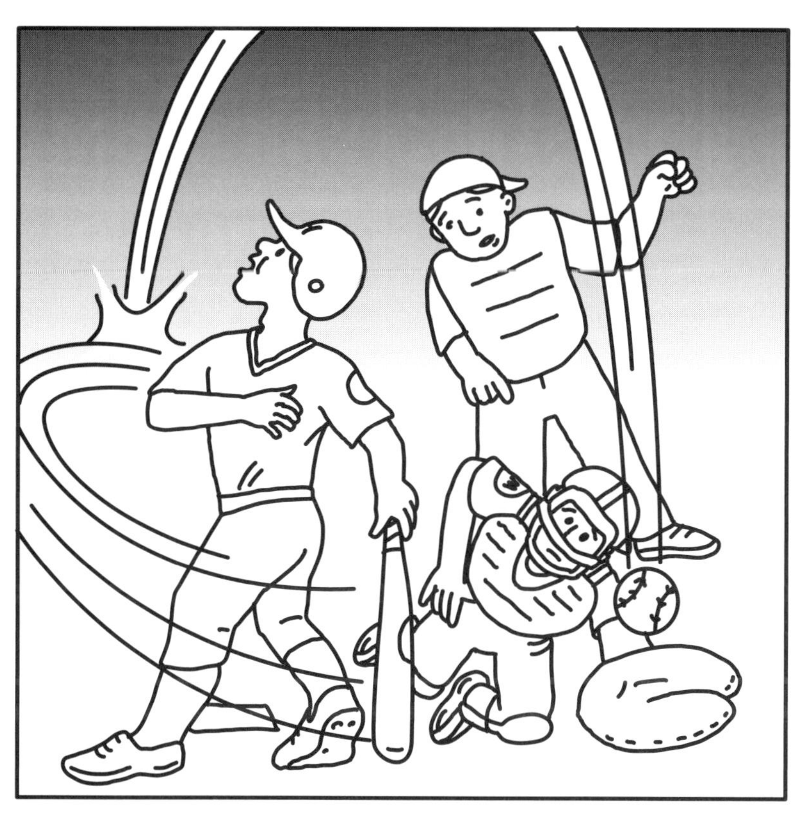

The next High Flyers
player hit a high pop-up
ball. The catcher got it.
"Two outs!" yelled
the umpire.

Dwight and his uncle
did high fives.
"That was a nice catch,"
Dwight said.

Then the pitcher for the
Mustangs struck out
the third hitter.
The High Flyers did not
score in the first inning.

Now the Mighty
Mustangs were
at bat. But they
did not score.

The next six innings
were just the same —
the Mustangs and the
Flyers did not score.
Dwight let out a sigh.

"We still have two innings," said Uncle Roy. "The Mustangs might win."
Dwight looked up at a bright star in the sky.

Dwight shut his eyes
tightly and made
a wish.

Soon it was the bottom of the last inning. The Mighty Mustangs were at bat.

The first Mustang player
held his bat high.
The pitch was good,
and he swung with all
his might. The ball
soared into the air.

13

Dwight saw the ball
as it came right to him.
He held up his glove
just in time.
"I have it! I have it!"
he yelled.

14

The fans were cheering.
Dwight was thrilled.
The hit was a home run!

"This is the best ending
ever," Uncle Roy said.
With a smile on his face,
Dwight looked up at that
bright star in the sky.